Heretic

Secrets of Socendor, Volume 1

Katherine Cook

Published by Arian Derwydd Books, LLC, 2023.

Secrets of Socendor, Book 1

The races of Socendor have coexisted on the continent for ages, but that is about to change. With the Koleri king dead, the heir to the throne, his son Breasal, sets up rule over the Koleri. His ambitions, however, go far beyond that, and his first target is the elven queen, Furia. Now it falls to an elven mage, Micheil, to rescue the queen and put an end to Breasal's reign.

Arian Derwydd Books, LLC
https://arianderwyddbooks.com/
Heretic
Copyright © 2022 by Katherine Cook
ISBN: 978-1-955467-80-3

Cast

King Amreth Vondrasek - Koleri king/Breasal's father

Queen Lisan Vondrasek (deceased)- Koleri queen/Breasal's mother

Vakis Izreih - Amreth's advisor

Lyvis Izreih - Vakis' brother

Braen Vondrasek - Breasal's son

Vamir - Vakis' son/Braen's closest friend/clandestine lover

Queen Furia - elven queen

Vanya - Furia's daughter

Lathai Thierauf (deceased) - Micheil's father

Vala Thierauf - Micheil's mother/elven mage

Micheil Thierauf - elven mage

Marilee Thierauf - Micheil's sister

Taeral - elven soldier/Micheil's lover

Soren Krelius - elven mage

Lerian - Furia's sister

Chapter One

"The king is dead."

The pronouncement echoed over the crowd below, and then the chatter began. Even from his vantage point on the balcony, Vakis Izreih could hear the prince's name roll through the crowd. Most of the people seemed apprehensive about the prospect of the prince taking the crown, but there were some who had been vocal throughout the last days of the king's life about Prince Breasal presenting a much stronger force in Socendor. Vakis dutifully kept his own misgivings to himself. King Amreth had been a kind and fair ruler. His son, however, had a reputation for cruelty and wielding an iron fist in every dealing that involved him – and several that did not.

It didn't matter. Vakis had served King Amreth faithfully, and he would do the same for the man's son.

Leaving the masses to their rumors, Vakis returned to the throne room. A part of him wasn't surprised to find Prince Breasal happily seated in the throne. Vakis bowed.

"So, my father is dead," Breasal said. He rubbed the polished wooden arms of what was now *his* throne. "Bury him beside his wife. Conduct whatever rituals you feel necessary."

"As you wish, Your Highness." The words tasted like ash, and speaking them aloud only increased the uneasiness in Vakis' mind. He bowed once more and left the room, wanting to put as much distance between them as he could.

Braen, Breasal's illegitimate son, fell into step beside him. The man had a habit of appearing out of nowhere. "You look like you've seen a ghost."

"Your father ordered the burial as soon as possible. Where is Vamir?"

Braen gestured in the direction of the servants' wing of the keep. "Last I saw him, he was grumbling about protocol."

"Tell him those protocols are in place for his – and *your* – protection. Your father would not tolerate your fraternizing with a commoner."

"I'm surprised my father even remembers I exist," Braen said.

Vakis sighed and stopped, as did Braen. "Regardless of how things are between you and King Breasal, you are his only heir. Keep up appearances no matter what happens. He will expect children from you, Braen."

One black eyebrow lifted, and Braen snorted. "Somehow, I don't think he's going to get any, unless your son's anatomy has changed within the past few hours."

Vakis immediately pressed a hand over Braen's mouth. "Hush! I don't care that you are sleeping with my son, but, rest assured, your father *will*. For all our sakes, keep your relationship with Vamir a secret. Do you understand?"

Braen nodded.

"Good." Vakis moved his hand. "I need to make preparations for the burial. Send Vamir to the burial grounds."

He left the young bastard princeling to it and continued to the front doors of the main keep. Before he reached them, the right one swung open. Vakis bit back what he truly wanted to say to the newcomer. Instead, he bowed. Lyvis, his brother, was a snake in Koleri clothing. Vakis didn't trust the man with a twig, much less anything of importance. Lyvis had always coveted Vakis' position in Amreth's court. That position, however, was now in contention. There was no guarantee Breasal would keep him on as advisor.

"Ah, just the man I wanted to see."

"What is it, Lyvis?"

Lyvis flipped a single silver coin, and Vakis caught it. "A token toward the good king's burial."

Despite his leeriness, Vakis nodded. "I will see that the priests make good use of it."

"Yes, yes." Lyvis waved him away. "I must speak with my king. Farewell."

Vakis watched him go, uneasiness filling the air. Lyvis was up to no good, as usual. Right now, though, Vakis just wanted to bury his king in honor. He feared the days of peace were at an end.

* * *

"Your father needs you."

"Of course, he does."

Braen chuckled and slapped the bare buttocks tempting him yet again. "We have, and I quote, 'appearances to maintain.'"

Vamir glanced over one shoulder before rolling his eyes. "I've heard that before, too." Still, he got up, giving Braen another chance to feast on the man's lithe form. "Keep looking at me like that, and we'll both be in trouble."

"Go," Braen said with a laugh and a gesture toward the door.

Vamir dressed, stole a quick kiss, and left Braen's room. Braen grumbled and sat on the bed. If it weren't for Vamir, he'd have left long ago. Surely, there were other Koleri out there who bore no love for what was sure to be a dark chapter in his people's history. He'd fought so long to gain his father's affections, but he realized he no longer cared. His duty was to his people, though, so he had no choice but to serve the throne – no matter who sat in it now.

Torn between wishing to honor his grandfather and serving his father, Braen figured it best to present a loyal front in the throne room. He straightened up his tunic and retied his hair before heading back out into the hall.

Servants bustled in various directions, some toward the great hall and others off to the cemetery. When he stepped into the throne room, there were several petitioners awaiting their chance to speak with their new king. Braen slipped off to the side to stand where Breasal once had. Breasal waved each person up, listened, and then muttered his instructions to an attendant. The attendant would then usher the petitioner off to another room to deal with whatever matter they had.

* * *

With Amreth buried, the king's court returned to its usual hustle, though an uneasiness had blanketed the entire keep. Braen hadn't seen anything personally, but rumors were rampant that his father had already begun the process of removing anyone loyal to Amreth. Braen caught Vamir's gaze from across the room. His lover seemed wary, looking furtively around the throne room. Only then did Braen realize that Vakis was nowhere in sight. Fear crept through Braen, from head to toe. Something felt very wrong.

Braen watched in silence for several minutes before he noticed Lyvis Izreih approaching the throne. Instead of waving him away, Breasal gestured for him to come closer. Lyvis bent to whisper in Braesal's ear. The smirk on the king's face made Braen's blood run cold.

A moment later, commotion sounded at the doors. Guards escorted someone inside, and it took all Braen had to remain upright. Vakis struggled against the hold the guards had on him.

Braesal motioned for the guards to move Vakis closer. When they did, others swooped in and pulled Vamir to the side. Breasal took a dagger and stepped down the dais to stop before Vakis. "Your services are no longer required," he said. Then he turned to Braen and held out the dagger. "Prove your loyalty, boy."

Braen began to shake, and he felt his last meal threaten its return. Breasal smiled - the first time Braen had ever seen him do so. "Your Highness..."

"Do you intend to serve your king?" Breasal asked. "Or will you join them? Relics of a dead king's rule?"

Braen took the dagger. Off to the side, Vamir screamed and struggled. Braen forced himself to block it out. He stood before Vakis. "I'm sorry."

Vakis, eyes full of tears, shook his head. "Don't do this, Braen. You are better than this."

"He is my king."

The second the blade cut into Vakis' flesh, blood pooled onto the stone floor. Braen dropped the dagger and walked away, sick and hating himself as much as he hated his father.

Chapter Two

"Please?"

Micheil Thierauf sighed and glanced over at his sister, Mari. "Vala will never agree to it."

Mari snorted and crossed her arms. Despite being nearly a foot shorter, she somehow managed to cow most people who argued with her. She wasn't conniving and secretive like their mother. No, Mari's ability lied in the way she smiled and the sparkle of joy in her eyes. No one in their right mind could deny her anything. Not even Micheil.

"All right. Pack quickly," Micheil said. "Say nothing to anyone."

Mari squealed, threw her arms around his neck in a hug, and then ran off to her rooms.

"Vala won't like it."

Micheil let his head fall back against the wall where he stood. "I know." He looked at the soldier across the hall from him. "If anyone asks..."

Taeral shrugged. "I'll say I have no idea where you went."

"Eventually, we will need to come up with better answers. I doubt our secret is still a secret."

Smiling, Taeral stepped closer, arms sliding around Micheil's waist. "And?"

"You may be a guard, but you are also still in line for the throne. Should it land on you to rule, you would be required to produce an heir."

"My grandmother will live forever, I think."

Micheil would've argued that sentiment, but a kiss silenced him. They didn't dare do anything in public, should anyone find out. Though he doubted the queen would've cared, her sister Lerian would gladly cause chaos if it meant possibly taking the throne out from under Furia.

Footsteps sounded, and a door opened further down the hallway. Taeral stepped back, smiled, and slipped out of sight through another door.

"There you are."

Micheil swallowed the groan before it escaped. He turned to face Vala. "Why are you looking for me?"

"Can I not see my son before I leave?"

Vala never did anything without a reason. Every word, every movement was calculated for a purpose. Children were supposed to trust their parents, but he couldn't recall a time when he had trusted her.

"What do you want?"

Giving up the façade of motherly love, Vala smirked. "I raised you well. Never trust anyone. At any rate, I leave at dawn. You will care for Marilee in my absence."

Micheil resisted the urge to tell her he had always cared for his sister, no matter where Vala went. "When are you to return?"

"I don't know," Vala said. "There are rumors the human king, Andrion, is in search of a court advisor."

"Will they even welcome an elf to such a position? Humans do not trust us. Relations between our races have always been strained."

"I have my ways," Vala said. "Glamour has its purpose. Remember that. I will be in touch." With that, she went back the way she'd come.

Micheil sighed. None of this boded well. Their family had no royal blood, and Micheil's position as head of the mages' guild only gave him so much sway over political matters. If Vala did anything to anger the humans, nothing Micheil could do or say would make a difference.

He went back to his own rooms to finish packing. Part of his job required reinforcing wards at various points throughout Cypravion. He enjoyed the quiet of the wilderness, far away from the bustle of Seriete and the court intrigue. He'd never taken Mari with him, but she was old enough now to start learning how to use her magic outside of the guild's confines. Though she was half-elven, she had inherited a good bit of Vala's natural talent for glamour. Perhaps he could help her hone those skills without the distractions of the city.

Pack slung over one shoulder, Micheil took a side exit from the keep in hopes of avoiding... well, everyone. When he reached the stables, he found Mari waiting in a corner with her mare, Stella. Micheil readied Aserion and led the stallion out of his stall.

"Do you remember the glen just west of the south gate?"

"Yes."

"Meet me there. Keep your hood up and your head down. Vala has already left, but she has eyes everywhere."

Mari nodded and mounted Stella. With a discreet wave of her hand, glamour settled over rider and horse, turning Stella's pristine white coat to a dark brown. Micheil watched them leave and hoped his sister's magic was strong enough to at least get out of the city. If Vala knew he was taking Mari from her guild studies, he'd never hear the end of it.

Getting out of the city proved uneventful, thank the gods. Micheil met Mari outside the walls. She'd let her glamour drop since outposts rarely had visitors. No one would know her, though they certainly knew Micheil. Mari guided Stella into step beside Aserion.

"You look pensive."

Micheil shook his head, unable to explain his bizarre thoughts of late. This was the only way they had a chance to talk without the possibility of Vala or one of her loyalists hearing them. "Something feels... wrong. Like a weight has fallen over Socendor."

"I know. I've felt it, too. You think Mother has anything to do with it?"

A part of him wanted to chuckle at the thought. It wouldn't be the first time Vala's managed to influence things outside of Cypravion. "Though I have no doubt she will eventually come into play somehow, no. This is far... darker, more oppressive than anything else I've ever felt. It's as if the land itself is waiting with bated breath for something to happen."

They fell into a companionable silence as they rode toward the first outpost. It was the only entry point between Cypravion and Akuron, where humans and Koleri kept generally peaceful existences. Elves had always stayed in Cypravion, away from the other races of Socendor. Although Seriete had a major port for trade with other lands of Peravon, Micheil's people remained fairly isolated out of choice. They distrusted others, sometimes to a fault.

The road to Midland Pass meandered through thick forests, south of Olvana River. By foot, the journey took two and a half days, but elven horses were known for their unnatural speed. As soon as the road's surface evened out, Micheil and Mari spurred their horses on. In the distance, Micheil spotted shadows in the trees, massive feralaan hunting prey. The cats were nearly as large as horses, and they were just as swift. They tended to leave travelers alone, unless some unlucky fool found himself lost in the woods. Feralaan occasionally chose a man or woman they deemed worthy, and the individual would have both a mount and a guardian for life. Unfortunately, they didn't share long lives with elves. Micheil's feralaan had passed ages ago. He still missed her at times.

They stopped at a small hunter's cabin along the road, about halfway to Midland Pass. Micheil fed both horses while Mari went inside and started the hearth fire.

As he began gathering wood for the fire and to replace what they used, Micheil pondered the odd feeling he'd been having lately. The atmosphere, even out here in the forest he loved so much, felt different, wrong. He wondered if maybe the humans had something to do with it. The Koleri had never given elves any trouble. Before he could come to anything resembling a possible answer, the thundering of hooves shook him out of his chaotic thoughts.

"Master Thierauf!"

Micheil turned to the rider, a young elven archer from Midland Pass. The rider's expression made it very clear this was no coincidence. "Yes?"

The rider guided his horse toward Micheil. "I am on my way to Seriete. The Koleri king has died."

King Amreth had been a kind and diplomatic ruler. If he was gone, the throne went to his heir, Breasal. Dread crept through Micheil. The answer to the uneasiness hit him full-force.

"Breasal has taken the throne."

The rider nodded. "Midland Pass is awaiting you."

"Has there been any sightings or stirrings from the Koleri or the humans in Akuron?"

"Not yet, but we have bolstered our numbers from outposts farther east."

"Good. Get to Seriete and inform Queen Furia. With Amreth dead, the peace in this land will fracture. His son will see to it."

"Yes, Master Thierauf."

Micheil watched the rider head down the road toward the city.

"Well, that explains it."

"It does indeed. My presence at the Pass is needed quickly." He faced Mari. "I don't want you in harm's way, Mari, should things deteriorate."

"I know." Mari stood on her tiptoes and kissed Micheil's cheek. "Please be safe. I'll go back to Seriete."

"I promise: we will venture out later, sometime."

"I'll hold you to that." With a smile, Mari went back into the cabin to gather her things. When she emerged once more, she waved at Micheil, mounted Stella, and started back home.

Micheil glanced in the direction of the mountains looming in the west. They separated Cypravion from Akuron, providing a natural defense. With Breasal on the throne, however, Micheil had the distinct feeling the mountains would provide little protection now.

Chapter Three

Braen had managed to stay out of his father's sight for the better part of the day. He'd lost the battle with his last meal hours ago, and even the smell of the evening supper from the kitchens made him sick. The servants avoided him, where before they had smiled and joked with him. He couldn't bear to even look at himself in his mirror. The thought of ending his life had crept up numerous times since Vakis' death.

Murder. Vakis' *murder.*

At Braen's hand.

Braen grabbed the nearest object and hurled it at the mirror across the room. The glass shattered and covered the floor in a thousand shards. Only then did Braen realized the thrown object was a book of lurid poetry, a gift from Vamir.

Though he hadn't heard anything concrete, Braen had no doubt Vamir had quickly joined his father in death. Breasal wouldn't have allowed him to live.

A knock startled Braen. So much for hiding.

"What?"

The door opened to reveal the king's snake. "Your king requires your presence, boy."

Braen scowled at Lyvis but stood anyway. "Inform him I'm on my way. Now remove your filthy, tainted hand from my door."

Smirking, Lyvis shut the door without another word. Braen would've thrown something else at it, but he simply didn't have the energy. Not for the first time, he wished he'd never been born to the monster now on the throne.

The moment he stepped out into the corridor, lingering servants scattered. Braen shoved down the surge of shame and continued to the throne room. Before he reached it, however, Lyvis appeared out of nowhere once again.

"War room. Now."

Braen didn't like the sound of that. He waited until Lyvis slunk back into shadows before he approached the closed door of the war room. He couldn't recall the last time anyone used it for its intended purpose. His grandfather had not been the warring type, preferring to rule with diplomacy. Breasal, however...

"Ah, there you are," Braesal announced by way of greeting when Braen opened the heavy wooden door. "You are to go to the elven capital of Seriete and meet with their queen."

Braen didn't dare ask why. "As you wish, Your Highness."

Breasal waved him away. "Then be off. Do not return without her."

Without her? How in the names of the gods was he going to convince the elven queen to even think about crossing the border into Akuron?

That question stayed at the forefront of Braen's mind as he left the keep and went to the stables. A small retinue of Koleri soldiers waited, Braen's horse ready. Out of the darkness of the stalls, Lyvis emerged. He handed Braen a ruby red vial.

"One drop, and she will be as pliant as a newborn babe. She will remain subdued long enough."

"Long enough for what?"

"To get her here, among many other things."

Braen's gut began twisting into knots again. "Will it kill her?"

"Oh, no. King Breasal has plans that require her to be alive. That is all you need to know."

When Lyvis left the stables, Braen studied the vial. The liquid in it had a dark tint, turning the red glass to the color of old blood. He tucked it into a pocket and took the reins from the soldier who held them. Without a word, he mounted his horse and didn't bother to wait for the others. He heard the hooves following him, and a part of him hoped maybe he could lose them outside the woods surrounding the palace.

Breasal had never liked the fact that Amreth built his keep so close to the human city of Akuron Heights, but the Koleri and humans held a relatively stable peace, even trading at times. Braen had the feeling that was going to change rather quickly now. It didn't explain the need for the elven queen, though. That was a mystery Braen wasn't sure he wanted to explore either. Magic ran strong in their family, and Breasal possessed far more skill at it than others. The notion that he had need of the queen didn't sit well with Braen.

As soon as they left the forest's cover, Braen felt the air shift. The woods were oppressive, but out here, he felt like he could breathe. The temptation to run filled him, but there was no point in doing so. Breasal would find him quite easily through blood and magic. Escape simply was not an option. Neither was defying the man's order.

The journey to Seriete generally took a few days, barring any unforeseen trouble. Getting through Akuron was the easy part. Braen dreaded entering the elven lands, though. Although they were not outright hostile toward Koleri, they were far from welcoming. The first major stop would be Midland Pass, the mountain outpost serving as the only easy access point between

Akuron and Cypravion. Although humans primarily controlled it, there were elves stationed within its walls. The human presence would probably keep any elven hostility at bay, but once through the pass, that changed. No humans ventured into Cypravion, and as far as Braen knew, elves didn't step foot in Akuron.

Overhead, dark clouds began to roll in from the south, beyond the jagged peaks of the Sunderlind Mountains. Sunderlind was a barren wasteland of scraggly plantlife and sand. No one lived there as far as Braen knew. Hell, he doubted *anything* lived there. The place was ill-suited for any sort of significant life.

As the darkness approached, he drew up his cloak hood and grumbled. He hated rain. When the first drops began to fall, the soldiers behind him echoed his sentiments. The road turned to a quagmire of mud and rock, but the horses made easy work of it. Although he preferred moving on foot and finding convenient places to take shelter, he didn't have that luxury now. Time was of the essence, and a horse would get him to Seriete quicker.

* * *

Aserion trotted into the courtyard at Midland Pass, barely showing any signs of fatigue. Micheil caught a few looks from the human soldiers, but no one approached him. He led Aserion to the stables and then headed toward a stone tower off to the side. Elves here kept their distance and watched over the area from vantage points in the mountains surrounding the pass. He stepped through the door, and the chatter fell silent.

"Master Thierauf," one of the elven soldiers called from where he sat at a table with others. "Captain Cail is in his office, waiting for you."

"Thank you." Micheil took the steps to the left up to the third floor of the building. At the top, he heard voices and knocked on the heavy wooden door.

"Enter."

He opened it and slipped inside, shutting it before speaking. "I expected more activity, given the circumstances."

"Hello to you, too, Master Thierauf," the captain said. He waved toward the other man in the room. "Meet Josiah Petiet, the human scout who brought us the news of King Amreth's death."

Micheil nodded in greeting. "Pleasure. I need to reinforce the wards. If something should happen—"

"What do you think will happen?" the captain asked. "I don't believe we have anything to be concerned with, to be honest. King Breasal has shown no aggression toward Akuron."

"My duty is to watch things from a magic perspective. He may not be actively planning anything on the surface, but believe me when I say that we should not discount his abilities to wreak havoc on these lands."

The captain smiled and stood. "Master Thierauf, please. Go rest yourself and do what you must for the wards. I assure you we are perfectly safe here. King Breasal has no intention of causing trouble in Akuron."

Micheil narrowed his eyes but decided to let it go for now. "As you say, Captain." He nodded in farewell to both men and left the room.

An uneasy feeling gnawed at him as he descended the steps. Captain Cail had never been quite so dismissive, and the lack of readiness in the outpost unnerved Micheil to no end. He ignored the rest of the men in the ground floor hall and stepped outside.

A newcomer shrouded in black rode into the courtyard from the Akuron gate, followed by a retinue of Koleri guards. The lead rider pushed back his hood, revealing an uncanny likeness to Breasal and the late king. Micheil watched the horseman dismount and disappear into the main outpost tower where the human officers met. The other Koleri riders remained on their horses, silent but ever watchful.

A minute later, the Koleri horseman emerged and rejoined his companions. An uneasy sensation swept through Micheil the moment he met the horseman's gaze. With a slight nod, the horseman and his companions left the outpost through the Cypravion gate. Micheil hurried to the officers' tower, the feeling in his gut growing into a knot of dread.

"Who was that?"

The two human officers seated at a long table looked up at him.

"Who?"

"The Koleri who was just in here," Micheil said.

The men looked at each other, then back to Micheil.

"There was no one in here," the man said. "We haven't had any visitors for days. Hell, your elves don't even show their faces around here."

Micheil stared at them in silence and left the tower without another word. Back outside, there was no evidence of the riders. No hoof prints in the dirt, no sign of anyone down the road past the Cypravion gate. The few soldiers milling about glanced at Micheil as if he'd lost his mind.

"Soldier, where did the Koleri riders go?" Micheil asked one before the man could duck into the barracks.

"What Koleri? The only riders we've seen in some time have been a few messengers from Akuron and, well, you."

A strong, dark magic was at play here. Something powerful enough to wipe the memories of everyone in the outpost, it seemed. And now the bearer of that magic was somewhere within Cypravion.

Wards forgotten, Micheil rushed back to the stables. Sensing his apprehension, Aserion awaited him near the gate, one hoof stamping the ground. As soon as Micheil settled into the saddle, Aserion took off through the gate, back toward Seriete.

* * *

"Who was that man?"

Braen shook his head. "I don't know, but it doesn't matter. No one in the outpost remembers us."

In truth, Braen was surprised his magic hadn't worked on the elf he'd seen. The others in the outpost had been easy enough to manipulate with a few muttered words and directed thoughts. The only reason he could figure for his magic not touching the elf was the possibility of the elf being a mage. He hoped the elven queen didn't possess much in the way of magic. Lack of resistance on her part meant an easier time for him.

He pulled out the map he'd stolen from the tower. Crudely drawn, it showed where the elven towns sat nestled in the thick forests. Better yet, the main road to Seriete had been plotted out with a few small notes about local wildlife – namely the feralaans that prowled the woods.

"Do not venture into the forest," Braen called back to the soldiers behind him. "Feralaans don't take kindly to anyone encroaching on their territory." He heard a few grumbles and smiled.

The massive cats rarely ventured through the mountains into Akuron, so sightings there were not common. Cypravion was their native land. The last thing Braen needed was to lose a soldier or two.

They rode for a few more hours before the men started on about rest. Braen didn't want to risk getting attacked by a feralaan or the elven mage reaching Seriete before they could. Still, he was tired as well. Spotting a small cabin ahead, he signaled to the soldiers. It was a risky move since he had no idea when someone would decide to stop at the same cabin.

While the soldiers tied their reins to nearby trees and headed into the cabin, Braen took a moment to surround the immediate area with a ward. The magic was rather rudimentary, but it would alert Braen of anyone entering the boundary he'd set. He hoped it would be enough warning should they be disturbed overnight.

Chapter Four

"Your Highness, I have received word that Braen has passed into Cypravion."

"Good," Breasal said. "Now tell me about this plan of yours. Are you certain it will work?"

Lyvis held up a scroll. "The spell is complicated and lengthy, but it will work. Any offspring will possess magic from you *and* Queen Furia."

"And the blood?"

"As it is with Braen, so shall it be with your new son," Lyvis said. "I daresay your child with the queen will be far more appreciative of it."

"Braen has his uses. Despite his lack of ambition, he has strong magic, whether he cares to wield it or not." Breasal leaned forward in his throne. "If this spell does not work, if it does not produce a male child, I will have you tortured and left to rot. Do I make myself clear?"

Lyvis swallowed but nodded. "It will not fail, Your Highness."

Breasal smiled and sat back. "For your sake, my friend, I hope not. Now go make my chambers ready for my future guest."

Lyvis bowed and hurried from the throne room. As soon as he was gone, Breasal waved over a guard.

"Ensure that everything is prepared," Breasal instructed. "Then take him to the dungeon."

"Yes, Your Highness."

The quicker he could get Lyvis out of the way, the better. The man was a weak link. With him gone, Breasal could focus solely on putting his plans into motion. Braen, while not sharing Breasal's appetite, indeed had his uses. Loyal to a fault, he was easily manipulated when it came to the preservation of his people. Breasal had learned over the years how to twist his first-born's compassion to his own needs. Now he just needed another son, one strong enough to bring all of Socendor to its knees.

* * *

Braen woke from a nightmare. He stood and went to the single window of the hunter's cabin that looked out onto the forest road. Memories and images replayed in his mind, most of them unpleasant. He didn't think he'd ever forgive himself for Vakis' death. The knowledge that Vamir had most likely met the same fate as his father only fueled Braen's self-loathing.

"What am I doing?" Braen muttered.

Not for the first time, he questioned his need for some sort of acknowledgment from Breasal, though he didn't quite know why. He couldn't bring himself to call the man 'Father.' He couldn't even recall a time when he'd felt anything resembling a familial connection. His mother had been a commoner, a mere dalliance for Breasal, and had died shortly after Braen's birth. For Braen, Amreth had been more of a father instead of a grandfather.

The sound of horse hooves thundering down the road jerked Braen out of his thoughts. He stepped to the side, out of view, just as a white horse galloped past the cabin. He recognized the rider as the elf he'd seen at the outpost. If the elf was returning to Seriete, it would hinder Braen's task of getting to the queen.

"Get up," he announced to the others in the cabin. "It is not yet dawn, but we must be moving. I fear we may have trouble in Seriete."

The others woke and readied themselves quickly and quietly. Braen headed outside and untied his horse from the tree. He mounted and set off, confident the guards would follow. He wasn't sure how far they were from Seriete, and he had no idea how he would even know the queen when he got there. He'd never seen her, and if she possessed magic as the elven rider obviously did, then she would certainly see him. None of it boded well, but he had a job to do.

* * *

Micheil dismounted and handed Aserion's reins to the stablehand, then he hurried into the palace. He'd seen through the glamour used at the hunter's cabin. Although he'd beaten the Koleri riders to Seriete, he had no doubt they would show up soon. Like many elves, Furia didn't possess magic. It was why Vala had been the queen's court mage, though the position now fell on Micheil. He stepped into the throne room, interrupting the queen's meeting with her other advisors

"Your Highness, I must speak with you."

Furia smiled and waved the others away. They left the throne room, but as Micheil approached the throne, Furia's smile faded.

"What's wrong?"

"I encountered a group of Koleri at Midland Pass," Micheil said. "No one remembered them."

Her brow furrowed. "What do you mean?"

"The men and elves stationed there claimed there *were* no Koleri. When I passed the hunter's cabin on the road, I saw through the Koleri's glamour. Your Highness, they are headed here, but for what purpose, I do not know. King Amreth is dead, and his son Breasal now sits on the throne."

"Are you certain of this?" Furia asked.

"Yes. Although I could be wrong, I don't think the Koleri are here diplomatically. The use of magic to make others forget them points to darker intentions."

Furia nodded. "I don't want to raise alarm among the citizens. Let them come here but watch them closely. Should you sense them use any sort of magic, can you counter it?"

"It depends on the magic," Micheil said with all honesty. "Breasal is rumored to practice magic involving the dead. Koleri are like us in that their magic follows bloodlines. If the rider I saw at Midland Pass is his son, then one can assume Breasal's magic was passed down."

"With Vala gone, I need you close by. The servants finished preparing her former chambers for you."

"And my sister?"

"She is most welcome as well. I know how much she means to you."

"Thank you, Your Highness. I will get her and our things settled, and then I will return to your side. We must make ready for the Koleri, no matter their motives."

Micheil left the throne room and headed to the home he shared with his sister. He found Mari nose-deep in a book. She looked up with a smile, but it faded quickly.

"What is it?"

"Get everything packed," he said. "We are moving into the keep. The queen wishes me to be closer at hand."

Mari stood and began gathering things as Micheil did the same. "What has happened?"

"There was a small group of Koleri at the pass," Micheil said while he placed books and jars into a wooden crate. "No one saw them but me. Whatever magic they used, it was strong enough to hide their movements. They are headed this way."

"What do you think they want?"

He stopped and set the crate on the table. Meeting Mari's gaze, he shook his head. "I don't know, and that is what worries me. Something looms in the air, Mari. I felt it on the road, and it permeated the pass. The Koleri are not coming to engage in diplomatic discussions."

Mari nodded and finished her own packing. She looked around the small house. "We grew up here."

"*You* grew up here," Micheil reminded her. "I know leaving it isn't easy."

"Have you thought about going to Akuron, like Mother?"

Micheil laughed. "Why would I? There is nothing for me there, nothing for you. Humans are not fond of elves, Mari."

She sighed. "I know. It's stupid, but I know."

Micheil stepped around the table and rested his hands on her shoulders, giving them a gentle squeeze. "You will find your purpose, Mari. I do not know where or when, but I promise you it is out there. Until then, I will do everything to protect you."

She smiled and hugged him. "Thank you."

Micheil kissed her hair. "I love you. You don't need to thank me."

Chapter Five

Glamour had its uses, but Braen figured it would be pointless here. Though he kept his hood up, as did his riders, he felt the weight of countless stares—none of them particularly friendly. Still, an uneasy peace remained between elves and Koleri, so he made it through Seriete's front gate with little trouble.

People lined the streets, stopped in their tracks as Braen rode down the main thoroughfare. Ahead, situated at the top of a small hill, sat the palace where Queen Furia ruled with a just, kind hand. At least that's what he'd always heard. He wondered if the elves would continue to see her in such a light once she joined forces with Breasal. Whatever happened, Braen had his orders: speak with her, orchestrate some time alone, and get her out without being caught.

As he approached the palace gate, he made a note of guards and potential exits. The elves were notoriously suspicious, but their lack of suitable protection around the queen's home shocked him. The elves had many things going for them as a race, but their pride alone would be their downfall.

Braen halted at the stables and dismounted. A nervous young groom took the reins, and Braen made his way to the main keep. Guards let him through after inspecting him for weapons. *At least they did that much.*

Braen maintained a neutral expression; although he didn't use it often, his magic remained his strongest weapon. The guards granted him entrance, and a page met him on the other side of the doors.

"Good afternoon and welcome to the court of Her Majesty Queen Furia. May I ask your name and purpose for this visit?"

Braen pushed his hood off, and gasps whispered around the room from where petitioners waited. "You may tell the queen Prince Braen Vondrasek comes on behalf of King Breasal of the Koleri on a matter of diplomatic relations."

"Y-yes, Your Highness."

The page opened the ornate wooden doors and bowed. When the gathering at the dais grew silent and looked his way, he announced, "Your Majesty, I present His Royal Highness Prince Braen Vondrasek, son of His Majesty King Breasal."

Braen ignored the temptation to roll his eyes. He'd never liked the pomp and circumstance of court, and neither had his grandfather. Breasal, however, relished it. At the queen's nod, Braen walked toward the dais. When he stopped before it, he gave her a slight bow, though obviously not enough of one as far as her attendants were concerned. Braen paid them no mind.

"Welcome to my court," Furia said. "I must admit, I am surprised to see a Koleri here. What news do you bring?"

"King Breasal wishes to speak with you regarding an alliance."

"I see. Does he foresee war with humans?"

"I can't speak to his exact reasons," Braen said. "I am here only as his envoy."

Furia waved her attendants away and stood. "Come with me, Prince Braen. We shall speak further in my private study."

Braen followed her, the queen paying no heed to the mutterings of her advisors and other attendants. She led him to a chamber overflowing with books, scrolls, and various trinkets and artifacts of elven history. She sat behind a gracefully carved desk and bade him to sit as well.

"Now, what sort of alliance does King Breasal offer?"

Braen gestured to his cloak. "May I?"

Furia nodded, and Braen brought out a small censer. He placed it on the floor and summoned just enough magic to light it. Smoke began flowing upward and soon formed a figure. The queen, like many other women, seemed utterly enraptured by Breasal, even if this image didn't quite match his true appearance.

"King Breasal offers his Koleri army, should you ever need it, in exchange for the same from the elves. His palace is open to you as well, should you desire to speak with him directly."

Furia tore her attention from the hazy visage and nodded. "I-I would like that, thank you. I will need to organize the journey and my time from the court, but you may tell him I would be honored."

Braen dismissed the smoke, and Furia shook her head slightly, as if trying to clear it. "I will inform him of this."

"Would you like a drink, Prince Braen?" Without waiting for him to answer, she stood and rounded the desk.

Braen got up and bowed. "Please, allow me, Your Majesty."

She smiled and gestured toward the cabinet on the far wall. "Thank you."

He went to the cabinet and took out two glasses. After pouring wine in both, he retrieved the vial hidden in his waist pouch and emptied it into her glass. He gave the glass a swirl and then returned to her. He handed the wine over and raised his own.

"To new alliances," he toasted.

"To new friends," she added.

He watched her as they both sipped their wine. He didn't know what to expect. She finished hers and stood once more.

"I will see you—"

She stumbled, and Braen caught her. Confusion marred her expression before her eyes closed. He placed her on a couch and went to find a servant.

"You, young man, I fear the queen is feeling a bit ill. She needs rest."

"Yes, sir!"

A moment later, several people filled the study. No one even glanced Braen's way as he sank into the shadows. Cloaked in glamour, he followed the group out and to the queen's chambers. He started to slip into her room, but an unwelcome sensation skittered up his spine. Cursing softly, he ducked into what turned out to be a storage room and watched through a tiny window in the door as the elf he'd seen at the pass hurried toward the queen's room.

That man was going to be a problem.

* * *

"What happened?"

"Master Thiefauf," one of the servants said, "the Koleri prince alerted us to her wellbeing. We brought her in here right away."

"Where is the Koleri?" Micheil asked. The servants looked around. Micheil sighed. "Find him. Now."

"Yes, Master Thierauf."

The servants left, and Micheil sat on a chair beside the bed. This was no ordinary illness.

"What did he give you?"

The queen's daughter, Vanya, entered and shut the door. "The guards..."

"They don't remember ever seeing any Koleri, do they?" He looked up at her.

Vanya shook her head. "How did you know?"

"I encountered the same magic at Midland Pass. Alert all guards in the city and send word to Midland Pass. The humans are far from reliable, but at least our own people there will be on the watch."

With a nod, Vanya left. Though she was the queen's daughter, she much preferred the simplicity of a guard's life over the court. Micheil didn't blame her one bit. He returned his attention to the sleeping queen. Whatever the Koleri prince had done, it was beyond Micheil's knowledge. All he could do was keep vigil until she woke.

* * *

Braen left his hiding spot in the storage room and scowled. That damned elf still sat in the queen's room. There had to be a way to get him out.

"Micheil!"

Braen barely had time to duck back inside before a young elven woman practically ran down the hall and flung open the queen's room door. From around her, Braen could see the bed. The elven mage who watched over the queen stood and ushered the young woman out into the hall. They stepped away from the door, giving Braen a clear shot if he could get by without being seen. Praying to any god that would listen, he summoned darkness around him, enveloping him in glamour. He darted from one room to the other.

It was now or never. He opened a window and peered out. A single story, but doable. He picked up the queen, reinforced his glamour for them both, and jumped to the courtyard below.

This whole damned plan had gone awry. Now he just had to make it to Breasal's palace in one piece.

Chapter Six

"Do not speak a word of this to anyone. Do I make myself clear?"

The advisors all nodded, but no one dared look Micheil in the eye. He caught sight of Taeral and waved him over.

"I need eyes everywhere. I want no part of Cypravion, Midland, or Socendor unwatched."

Taeral nodded. "Where will you be?"

"I am riding to the Koleri palace. Gather a small force and meet me outside the city gates. Her advisors have been instructed to keep this quiet for now. Vanya is acting as regent in her mother's absence."

"You know this may lead to another war."

Micheil sighed. "It's possible, but if we don't get Furia back, that possibility turns into a guarantee. Go. I'll meet you outside."

"Master Thierauf, Princess Vanya wishes to speak with you."

Micheil headed into the throne room. He barely got through the door before Vanya stormed over to him, absolutely incensed.

"I'll kill that bastard myself! Where is he?"

"I don't know. I'm taking a small contingent to Breasal's palace. I will bring her back, Vanya. I promise."

Tears threatened in her eyes, but she didn't let them fall. "You had better."

Micheil left the palace and headed straight for the stables. A groom had Aserion saddled and ready, most likely at Taeral's bidding. Micheil hurried out of the city and met the others just beyond the main gate.

"Orders?" Taeral asked.

"Keep your wits about you. Koleri have no qualms about using manipulation over others. We are going to get the queen—not to start a war."

Taeral didn't seem very convinced, but he kept his thoughts to himself. They could discuss it later. Micheil led the way, but Taeral quickly matched him in pace.

"This is going to end badly. You know that, yes?"

After a moment, Micheil answered, "yes. I don't know why the prince took her, but rest assured Breasal has plans for our queen. What they are, I don't know."

"What do you intend to do?"

"I hope to remain as diplomatic as possible. We will see soon enough just how successful that will be."

* * *

"Eat. You must be hungry."

Furia glared at the young man who stood guard at the door. "I will take nothing you or your king offer."

"As you wish, Your Highness. I believe, however, that you will change your stance in time. King Breasal is a reasonable man."

"Reasonable?" Furia shot to her feet and stormed over to the guard until she was inches from his face. "His son abducted me through nefarious magic. How is that reasonable?"

The guard didn't move her away or really even change expressions. "Prince Braen's actions were... unfortunate. King Breasal simply wishes to discuss diplomatic arrangements with you. Nothing more."

Furia would've happily argued, but a knock on the door stopped her. The guard opened the door. Furia expected a servant, page, or maybe even that damned prince. She hadn't planned on coming face to face with the Koleri king—not like this, anyway.

"Good afternoon, Your Highness. I trust my men have treated you well."

Lost in eyes the color of the roses in her garden, Furia found herself unable to speak for a moment.

King Breasal smiled—the first actual smile she'd seen since his son stepped foot in her throne room. "Won't you please join me for the midday meal? We have much to discuss."

She shook her head to clear the fog. "I want to go home."

"You will be given a full escort back, of course. It will take time to arrange it, however, so will you join me in the meantime?"

He offered his arm to her. After a few seconds, she accepted. They left the room and headed toward what she assumed to be the dining hall. There was no throne, no dais—just several wooden tables lining either side, with a single table at the head to look out over the others. He led her to this table and even slid her chair out for her. Once she was seated, he took his own beside her. Then servants began filing in, each one carrying a tray of food. Another appeared to her right and offered to fill her cup.

Fruits, breads, meats, and cheeses soon covered the table. Breasal took it upon himself to place a bit of each on Furia's plate before getting his own. Only after the servants left did he speak.

"I do apologize for the manner in which you arrived. I wish you no harm, Your Highness."

Furia stared at the food on her plate. She waited until he began eating before she even touched a single morsel. "Why am I here? I told him I would enjoy the chance to speak with you, but I fully intended to do so on my own terms."

"I will be direct, as you seem to be the type of person who appreciates it. I have no heirs beyond Braen, and he is not fit for rulership. He is weak-willed and does not possess the mettle that being a king requires. Word is that your daughter Vanya has no desire to hold court either."

Furia nibbled on a slice of bread. "That is true, but what does your situation have to do with me?"

Breasal placed a scroll on the table. "I am offering my son as a suitor to your daughter. Their union would build a bridge between our people and cement our own lines on the thrones for ages to come."

Furia nearly choked on a sip of wine. "You are truly mad. Vanya is headstrong and would do no such thing."

"I understand your hesitation. Braen is a bit unconventional, to say the least. That said, I believe he can be persuaded."

"Vanya will not," Furia said. "Believe me, I have tried. I would love grandchildren."

Breasal chuckled. The soft sound seemed to fill the air around them with its own sort of enchantment. Furia looked away from him when she felt her cheeks grow warm. She needed to get away from this man. Every second near him chipped away at her resolve, and she had no idea why.

They finished eating in silence, and a servant returned to refill their wine. Collecting his cup and hers, Breasal stood and offered his arm once more.

"Shall we take a walk? You are not a prisoner here, and I would like you to feel more comfortable during your stay."

Furia hesitated only for a moment before accepting. She sipped her wine as they strolled out into the courtyard. Breasal's palace was situated in Ronu Wood, a forest south of the human capital of Akuron Heights. Koleri had no land to call their own. Humans outnumbered them here, and elves had no intentions of sharing Cypravion.

Breasal remained silent as they walked, leaving Furia to further wonder about what sort of man he truly was. She'd heard stories, of course, but none of them fit the Koleri ruler. She soon found herself laughing when he started telling her stories of his childhood here.

By the time they reached her room, Furia felt more at ease with him than she had her late husband. So when Breasal kissed her, she didn't resist. In fact... she welcomed it.

"Rest, Your Highness. We can talk more tomorrow."

"Wait." She caught his hand and stared down at their linked fingers, hers pale, his pitch black. "Don't go."

Breasal smiled.

"I don't know why, but I feel... something," Furia admitted. "I would like to spend more time with you."

Breasal opened the door and bowed. "As you wish, Your Highness. I am yours for the evening, if that is what you want."

Keeping his hand in hers, Furia entered the room, pulling the Koleri with her. He shut the door and locked it. She released him and turned before unclipping her cloak. "It is."

"Please, allow me, Your Highness."

"Furia." She took another kiss and whispered, "please call me Furia."

* * *

Braen stayed out of sight, but he'd heard everything. The notion of marrying made him a bit ill, but watching his father seduce the elven queen so quickly was far worse. Not for the first time, Braen missed his grandfather. Amreth had been kind and didn't use magic for anything other than amusing children. Breasal's blatant sorcery on the elven queen didn't sit well with Braen. Whatever his father had planned, Braen realized he wanted nothing to do with it any longer.

He retreated to his own room and pondered his next steps. He couldn't stay here, especially when the elves came for their queen. He sat at his table and sighed. He had no where to go. At one time, he'd found refuge from his father and the court in Vamir's arms, but that was gone now. It hadn't been love, but he'd cared for Vamir greatly. Now he had no one to go to, no place in which to hide. If he did, he figured his father would find him anyway—if not by magic, then by the damned dragon's blood that ran through their cursed veins.

By the time he had formulated a plan of heading into the mountains, the sun had begun to dip below the horizon. He couldn't wait any longer.

Braen grabbed the bag he'd packed months ago, when Amreth had initially fallen ill. Then he slipped out of the palace and made his way to the stables. Thunder echoed through the woods. He barely managed to cloak himself in glamour before a contingent of elves barreled into the inner bailey. Led by the elf he'd encountered at Seriete, the group stopped at the doors of the palace, and without waiting for the guards to react, strode right in with a wave of the leader's hand.

This didn't bode well at all.

Chapter Seven

As much as he would love to storm into the bastard's throne room, sword drawn and magic at the ready, Micheil stayed his hand and waited while the page announced him. He'd half expected Breasal to deny him entrance, but the page stepped to the side when the Koleri king bade them to enter.

Micheil held his tongue until he reached the dais. "Where is Queen Furia?"

Breasal's smile may have worked on Furia, who didn't possess magic herself, but Micheil was unphased. "She is here and quite well. My dear queen, you have visitors."

Furia stepped out of a doorway at the side, looking none the worse for wear. "Micheil. I didn't expect you."

Micheil bowed to her. "Your Highness, may we have a moment alone?"

Furia looked at Breasal, who nodded in agreement. Then she joined Micheil, taking the arm he offered. He led her away from the dais and stopped just outside the throne room doors.

"We must get you out of here," Micheil whispered, wary of eavesdroppers.

"I understand your concern, but King Breasal has been very kind and accommodating. I am fine, Micheil."

None of this was right. He glanced around, then whispered while brushing his hand down her face. Furia blinked and shook her head. Then she surveyed their surroundings.

"Micheil... where...?"

"It's a long story, Your Highness. We need to get you home."

"I remember the prince coming to see me, but nothing else until last night."

"Last night?"

Furia met his gaze, a mix of sorrow and fear in her eyes. "Micheil... we..." She placed a hand on her belly.

Cold swept up Micheil's spine, but he didn't dare say a word. "We can deal with that when we get away from here."

"He will find me."

"And he will find *me* waiting for him," Micheil countered. "My men are in the stables."

She looked back at the closed throne room doors, then to Micheil. "Okay. I am ready."

Her hand in his, Micheil searched for another exit. A figure stepped out into the hallway they were in, and Micheil drew his sword.

"One more step," Micheil warned.

The figure shoved a hood back, and Furia gasped.

"You abducted my queen. I should kill you where you stand."

"If you follow me, I can lead you to your men without guards spotting you."

"Why should we trust you?"

The prince gave them a slight smile. "You can't. I wouldn't. But I also can't stay here any longer. My father sees me as a worthless pariah, so I am leaving as well."

Praying he wasn't making a huge mistake, Micheil sheathed his sword. Furia's hand tightened on his. "Very well. We will follow you, but rest assured, I won't hesitate to kill you if I must."

"Understood. This way."

* * *

Braen remained in the shadows and watched the elves ride away with their queen. He had no idea if his father had intended to release her, but it was too late now. He left his hiding spot and made his way to a smaller side exit out of the courtyard.

"He will have your head for that."

Braen stopped and sighed. "I know." He turned to face Renir, a hunter he'd befriended years ago. "Whatever my father has planned will not end well. I want no part of it."

"Where will you go?"

"The mountains, at least far enough away that finding me will take more time and resources than he cares to use."

Renir shifted his bow on his shoulder. "Very well. Lead on."

"Renir—"

"Look, I trust Breasal as far as I can throw him," Renir said. "You, on the other hand, have been a friend to me for quite some time. Two will survive in the wild better than one."

"All right, come on. I could use the company."

Grateful for the companionship, Braen started into the woods, Renir behind him. Having a skilled hunter would come in handy since any use of magic could potentially give their location away. The mountains loomed in the distance, promising an escape from the hell Breasal had most likely unleashed by sleeping with the elven queen. Koleri and elves were never meant to produce offspring. The idea that Breasal had done it, using his magic to supplement the process, chilled Braen to the bone. If the child survived infancy, Braen pitied the poor creature.

* * *

Thanking the gods for the uncanny speed of elven horses, Micheil kept one arm tight around Furia's waist as they rushed through Akuron toward Midland Pass. They would be safe once they reached Cypravion. Furia dozed, and he took comfort in that. Her womb now bore what could possibly be the greatest threat Socendor had ever seen. Should the babe live, no one in Socendor could know the truth.

Midland Pass came into view, and soon they were riding through the gate. Micheil didn't dismount when the others did, however. Taeral walked over and rested a hand on Micheil's thigh.

"Rest, then continue on. I have to get her home."

Taeral nodded. "We are at war, you know. He will come for her."

"It's certainly possible."

"How did you get her out of the palace?"

Micheil wondered if he should say anything, but he and Taeral didn't keep secrets from one another. "The prince."

"What?"

"Prince Braen aided us," Micheil said. "Most likely at his own peril. He chose exile rather than remain with his king."

"Interesting." Taeral patted Micheil's leg. "Get home. I will see you soon."

Micheil bent down for a quick kiss, then nudged Aserion onward. The sooner they reached Seriete, the better.

Chapter Eight

Braen tossed a pinecone onto the fire and watched the flames spit and sizzle. Sparks floated up into the air amid the smoke then died out. His thoughts came and went, but nothing stuck long enough for him to really focus. A part of him missed home already, but he didn't dare show his face there again.

"Eat."

"I'm not hungry."

"You'll need it once we get up into the caves," Renir said.

"I'm still not sure if the caves are the best idea. All manner of things live in the mountains, and he'll sense it if I use even the slightest bit of magic."

Renir sat down beside Braen and sighed. "I know, but we have little choice. We can't go east to Midland. Elves and humans will not take kindly to our presence, especially now."

"The only elf I'd worry about in Midland is probably on his way to Seriete with his queen. I highly doubt they stopped in the Pass for anything."

"What did your father want with her anyway?"

Braen wondered at the wisdom of saying a word about it, but the implications of Breasal's actions would be felt all over Socendor the moment the queen gave birth. "He did the unthinkable. I don't know if the baby will survive infancy, given the magic used to conceive him, but should the child live..."

"Oh, gods," Renir muttered. "Why? What was he thinking? What is his plan?"

"Subjugation, I imagine," Braen said. "My father craves control over everyone and everything."

"What about the humans? Why not go for them first?"

"They don't possess magic, so they don't pose the most immediate threat. If Breasal gains control of the elves somehow, the humans of Socendor don't stand a chance against him."

A twig snapped, alerting them both. Renir shot to his feet, bow at the ready in the blink of an eye before Braen could even unsheathe his daggers. A figure emerged from the brush, and Braen let out a sigh of relief. Renir relaxed and lowered his weapon.

"Elia? What are you doing here?" Renir asked the young Koleri woman.

She approached the fire, one hand resting on the hilt of her own dagger. "Breasal has sent scouts to find you," she said to Braen. "I came to warn you. What did you do?"

"I let them take the queen," Braen said. "What's done is done."

Elia eased her defensive stance and sat on a stone near the fire. "I overheard him speaking with someone. The queen's 'escape' was intentional. He allowed the elves to take her. He said the magic is done, and the plan is in motion. He instructed the scouts he sent for you to not harm you."

Braen didn't believe that for a second. Breasal would gladly kill him to get rid of potential competition with the poor soul the elven queen now bore. "I'm not going back. I'll fight the scouts, to the death if need be, but I refuse to step foot anywhere near my father's palace now."

"I figured as much," Elia said. "It's why I packed what I needed, knowing I wouldn't be returning either."

"Elia—"

"Look, your father is insane," she said, cutting Braen off before he could continue his argument. "Even the people know that. Word around the palace is that not everyone wants him on the throne. Many are leaving for Sunderlind."

"Sunderlind?" Renir asked. "It's a wasteland. They can't survive there."

Elia shrugged. "Doesn't mean they won't try. Desperation drives them. They fear Breasal and what he can do."

Braen weighed their options. Despite being an arid, sandy place, Sunderlind could be defended in the right locations. "All right. We will go."

"What?" Renir asked him, incredulous. "You can't be serious."

"What choice do we have? My father is hellbent on starting a war with the elves and possibly the humans. At least in Sunderlind, we—and our people—stand a chance of escaping the devastation to follow."

Renir and Elia exchanged glances before Renir looked back to Braen. "Then we are with you."

"Thank you," Braen said. "I'm going to need all the help I can get, I fear."

* * *

Furia stared out the window, unmoving. She'd done little else since they arrived back home. Micheil had done everything he could to settle her mind, but he feared nothing would ever be the same. He felt helpless, a sensation he did not enjoy. He set the tray of food on the table in her outer chambers and left. There was nothing else he could do, so he returned to the throne room.

Advisors clustered near the dais, and Vanya had vacated the room the moment Micheil and Furia had returned. Before he had a chance to say a word, one of the advisors rushed over to him.

"Master Thierauf, how is she?"

"Queen Furia is feeling unwell, but she will return to her duties soon. In the meantime, all concerns may be directed to me. I think Vanya has had her fill of the court."

Satisfied, the advisor went back to the others to relay the news. Micheil despised the court almost as much as Vanya, but as the queen's right hand in terms of magic, he had little choice but to remain available. He sat in the chair he used during Furia's sessions and let his head fall back against the wall. He closed his eyes and just let his mind slip away, far from the worries now plaguing them all.

* * *

Fire. Smoke. Death.

"From the depths of the earth and the sea,
The endless skies and the mists of time,
I call thee, beasts of fire..."

A young man, with hair as black as midnight, stood on a hilltop, his arms raised to the swirling forms above him. In and out of the voluminous clouds, great beasts flew. Fiery plumes of red and orange surrounded the behemoths, and their obsidian scales glimmered in the silver moonlight as it cascaded down onto the valleys and hills.

"You are in danger," Micheil warned from below.

"As are you. You are mine. For that, you will be hunted."

* * *

"Micheil?"

A voice broke the uneasy spell, waking Micheil from... a dream? A premonition? He didn't know. He wasn't sure he *wanted* to know.

"Yes?" He looked up at his sister, who studied him with a worried expression. "I'm fine."

Mari raised one eyebrow but didn't press the matter. "I've moved everything I want to keep into my chambers beside yours. Must I really remain in the palace?"

"I know you don't want to, but it's for your safety. Vala's reputation isn't the best, even among our own people. She may be gone, but there are those who would not hesitate to harass you."

"All I have to do is remind them my brother is a brooding, overprotective ass who will happily zap them into oblivion."

Micheil sighed. "Fine. But please be back by nightfall, for your brooding, overprotective brother's sake."

She grinned and bent down to kiss his cheek. "See you later, my beloved grumpy one."

He watched her leave and wondered if maybe he *was* a bit strict. Vala had made many enemies, and only Micheil's position as the queen's magic advisor kept quite a few people from giving him and Mari hell. Mari's human parentage didn't help matters. Elves, for all their love of beauty, were quite stubborn in accepting others who weren't pure elves.

"Your Highness!"

At one of the advisors' pronouncement, Micheil stood and met Furia halfway to the throne. She ignored all others and focused solely on Micheil.

"I have no magic," she whispered. "I want him shielded, his identity concealed."

Micheil didn't need to ask who. "To truly hide his lineage, the magic must be permanent, Your Highness."

"No one can ever know the truth. Not even him."

"How do you know the child is male?"

Furia discretely rested a hand on her belly. "I just... know. I think his father used magic to ensure it."

Despite the dread creeping through him at that prospect, Micheil nodded. "Then it will be done, Your Highness. No one will ever know."

"Thank you."

Chapter Nine

The spell Furia wanted was complicated, and Micheil had sent her to her chambers while he prepared what he needed for it. He found the jar with the last of his winterclove and scooped a spoonful into the bubbling water hanging over the hearth. The concoction wasn't as vile as some he'd made in the past, so getting her to drink it shouldn't be an issue. He could have easily cast a quick spell in any other situation, but this one had to be stronger... and permanent. He couldn't risk it potentially breaking should Breasal find out.

"*Haina hair fruun llusayas.*"

Hide his blood forever.

Micheil closed his eyes and prayed with every fiber of his being his magic would do just that for the poor child Furia now carried. The possibility of ending the pregnancy had not been an option. Furia would never do it, and Micheil could never bring himself to aid in such a spell. He'd been asked by other women in the past, but he'd simply directed them to his fellow mages. He placed his thoughts on the subject squarely on Mari. Vala had wanted to end that pregnancy, but Micheil had begged her not to as he had longed for a sibling.

A knock on the door drew him out of his thoughts.

"Come in."

Furia entered and shut the door quietly behind her. "Are you ready?"

"I am." He tipped the pot just enough to pour the mixture into a cup. He infused it with a little magic to cool it and handed it to her. "The taste isn't terrible, and you must drink it all. Once you're done, lie down, and I'll finish the spell."

Furia stared into the cup, gave it a swirl to help cool it a bit more, and took a sip. "It's a bit sweet."

"Winterclove," Micheil said.

Nodding, she finished the drink and set the cup on his table. Then she went to his bed. He waited until she got comfortable before he pulled a chair to the bedside.

"May I?" he asked, gesturing to her belly. She nodded, and he placed his hands over her, just barely touching.

Eyes closed, he focused his thoughts on the child now growing inside her. He wrapped the boy in his magic, swathed in the brilliant emerald green of the Cypravion forests just beyond their city. His magic had always been that of healing and aiding, and he poured every ounce of it into the baby just beneath his palms. Green surrounded his hands and spilled out to encompass Furia and himself. No matter what happened, no matter where their lives led, he was now bound to this child on a soul-deep level he'd never felt before.

The light faded, and Micheil sat back in the chair. An unnamable sensation swept through him, unlike anything he'd experienced with any other magic.

"Micheil?"

"I am fine," he lied. He gave her a smile, but her expression made it quite clear she saw right through it. "Trust me. The spell is set and can't be broken. Not even by Breasal."

"Thank you."

"You are quite welcome. If you will excuse me, though, I need a bit of rest."

"Of course." She stood and put a hand on his shoulder, giving it a gentle squeeze. Then she left his room.

Micheil crawled onto the bed, mind in turmoil. The spell had been successful, but he had no idea what to make of the effects lingering within himself. He allowed sleep to take him, grateful for the peace.

* * *

Warmth against him woke Micheil from a deep sleep. He managed to summon a smile and placed his hand on Taeral's where it lay on his hip. Taeral's grip tightened a little.

"Are you all right?"

How did he answer? Micheil didn't know how to explain it. Taeral possessed no magic.

"I... don't know. The spell is done."

A gentle nudge urged him to roll over and meet a concerned gaze. As a soldier, Taeral knew danger and fear quite well, but this was something Micheil couldn't begin to express. As if to let the matter go for now, Taeral simply leaned down for a kiss. Micheil lost himself in it, as much as he could. He adored the man, but something had changed, something not even Micheil understood. Still, the hand moving to his thigh managed to chase away those thoughts for now.

"I won't pretend to understand," Taeral murmured as he kissed a path along Micheil's jaw and down his neck. "Just let me ease your cares for a while."

In answer, Micheil moved Taeral's hand closer to where he really wanted it and parted his thighs. A firm squeeze stole his breath, and Micheil whispered his lover's name.

Taeral hummed in agreement and worked his way down. He pushed Micheil's shirt up and peppered the skin beneath with kisses. Then those calloused, warrior's hands rid Micheil of his pants. A moment later, heat enveloped Micheil, stealing his breath and his wits. He threaded his fingers through his lover's hair and held it out of the way while Taeral toyed and pleasured him with mouth and tongue.

Just before Micheil thought he would climax, Taeral pulled away. Micheil groaned but knew more awaited him. He opened his legs and moaned Taeral's name as slick fingers entered his body. Taeral's lips met his own, and then the warrior filled him completely. Micheil let himself finally relax for the first time in days, and Taeral loved him until they both were well and truly spent.

* * *

Braen tossed a pinecone onto the fire and watched it spark. Renir and Elia still slept, though they'd moved closer to one another during the chilly night. He couldn't help but smile a little. Renir had confessed quite a few times about his feelings for Elia. Perhaps they could find some happiness now, far from the hell of Breasal's rule. For himself, Braen refused to even consider such a thing. He'd all but ensured Vamir's death without lifting a finger. Not for the first time since leaving the palace, he contemplated sneaking away into the mountains to face whatever creatures dwelt in their depths. He wasn't entirely sure what stopped him from doing it.

Elia stirred and eventually sat up. She blinked at Braen and glanced outside.

"Dawn is not far off."

"Have you not slept?" she asked.

Braen shook his head. "No. I'm not certain I will ever sleep in peace again."

She rummaged in her pack and handed him a cluster of berries. Then she moved over and sat beside him. "Vamir?"

He nodded and popped a berry in his mouth.

"His fate was out of your hands."

"I murdered his father," Braen muttered. "In front of him. Even if he didn't meet the same fate, that is something no one would ever forgive."

"I am sorry."

"You have nothing to apologize for, but thank you." He focused on the slowly growing light outside. "My father will not stop until all who were loyal to Amreth are dead."

"Sunderlind may be our only option," Elia said in between berries. "I don't like it anymore than you do, but what other choice do we have?"

"None," Braen said. "You said people were leaving?"

Elia nodded and ate another berry. "Small groups, as if they were trying to be inconspicuous about it, lest Breasal find out. I heard most were taking some of the wilder paths through the mountains, but others talked about the caves."

"They won't make it. If the wildlife on the mountains don't kill them, the creatures beneath most certainly will."

"You mean dragons? Are they real?"

Braen wondered at the wisdom of showing her just how real they were. He figured, should they do battle together, she would discover it anyway. He drew his dagger and cut his palm. Elia gasped the moment his tainted blood sizzled on the stone cave floor. He expended just enough magic to heal the wound quickly.

"When he was younger, my father learned that dragon blood would strengthen his magic should he drink it. It nearly killed him, and he murdered the mage who'd given him the idea, but it worked. Unfortunately, it was passed down to me when he impregnated my mother."

"That explains why you always wear gloves and full leather armor when sparring."

Braen looked to see Renir watching them. He nodded. "Indeed. My father kept it a secret, as did I. I would prefer it remain that way."

"No one will hear it from us," Elia said. She tossed her pack to Renir, who looked through it for food.

"I am assuming we are going to Sunderlind," Renir said before taking a bite of bread he'd found. At Braen's nod, he added, "is that wise?"

"Wiser than returning to my father's palace," Braen pointed out. "Though I worry for the people who are leaving as well. The mountains—especially the caves—are not safe."

"The only other route is through Midland Pass and into Cypravion," Renir said. "And that is out of the question."

Braen thought of the elven mage he'd seen numerous times. He had a nagging feeling they'd cross paths again soon enough. "We need to find the groups and help them all reach Sunderlind safely. There are places along the base of the mountains where a few crops can grow, and the coast should prove fruitful for fishing. I suggest we look there for places to settle."

"Agreed," Renir said. "I'll get things packed up."

Elia stood to help him. From the corner of his eye, Braen watched them share a quick kiss. At least someone managed to find a bit of happiness in this damned nightmare.

Chapter Ten

Micheil,

I am quite settled here in King Andrion's court. He even put me in one of the towers within the main keep, much to his wife's chagrin. It is no matter. I have his ear far more than she ever will.

I trust affairs are in order with you and Mari. Has Furia moved you into the palace? She remarked on her intent to do so before I left. I assume Mari's studies are progressing as well. She possesses my talent, after all. She is well-suited to take over as the queen's magical advisor while you focus on your guild duties.

Speaking of duties, I have sent word for one of my more promising pupils to join you. He has spent some time here in Akuron Heights, but he still has much to learn. I am entrusting you with his instruction. His name is Soren. See to it he joins the guild with honors. I'm sure, as the master, you can do so without much opposition.

Give my regards to the queen.

-V

Micheil raked a hand through his hair and set the letter on the table. Vala had wasted absolutely no time digging into the human king's affairs. Not that Micheil was surprised. Vala was indeed talented as a mage, but she was also ruthless and conniving, able to twist words and thoughts to her advantage. And a pupil? Micheil had thought she'd given up on teaching anyone ages ago. He vaguely remembered the name Soren, but he couldn't recall a face to match it.

"Micheil?"

He handed the missive to his sister and sat down. As she read it, he poured them both wine. She chuckled and joined him, placing the paper facedown, as if to hide its contents. She'd learned several years ago that Vala had zero maternal instincts and cared only for herself.

"Soren? Do you know him?"

Micheil slid her cup to her and took a sip from his own. "The name sounds familiar, but Vala hasn't had a student in a very long time. If he learned from her, only time will tell if he shares her mannerisms."

Mari drank her wine but looked pensive. Micheil waited patiently for her to speak.

"You've changed."

He smirked and finished his drink. "Is it that obvious?"

"To me," she said. "Micheil, what is it?"

"I don't know," he admitted. "I wish I had an answer for you. Taeral said the same thing last night. I didn't have an explanation for him either."

"How is he? I haven't seen him much lately."

"With the death of King Amreth, and Furia's situation, the military has been on high alert. He runs between posts to relieve other soldiers. I'm surprised he was able to go with me to get her from Akuron, to be honest."

Mari sighed. "What will become of the... baby?"

"The child's identity is hidden, and it will remain so for his entire life. Breasal has strong magic, but so do I. Furia has talked about sending the boy to Akuron Heights when he is born."

"She knows the baby will be a boy?"

"She believes Breasal used magic to ensure it," Micheil said. "Koleri, like the humans, follow the father's bloodline when it comes to the throne. So a son will inherit before a daughter will. Not to mention, Breasal has no other children."

"What about the prince? The one who came here?"

Micheil thought about the Koleri he'd seen numerous times. "He is Breasal's son, yes, but from what I've gathered, his mother was a commoner. Koleri frown on such things."

"So was my father," Mari pointed out.

"True, but elves don't care. Well, most of us don't. I'm sure Lerian would gladly protest should Furia die. Vanya may be Furia's daughter, but her father was a soldier—not royalty. I fear Lerian would use that fact to sway others into letting her take the throne."

"Vanya doesn't want it anyway."

Micheil sighed. "Believe me, I know."

* * *

Braen wondered, not for the first time, if this was a good idea. They'd found three small groups heading through the mountains and had merged them. Unfortunately, whether he liked it or not, those people now looked to *him* for guidance.

"We must find the others," Braen said to the nearly two dozen Koleri before him. "If anyone dares to attempt the caves, they will not survive."

"I heard some were going to come this way first," one of the men said. "Look for a passage over the mountains before resorting to the cave systems."

Braen nodded. "Then we need to set up camp along the most likely routes. There is safety in numbers, so no one should be alone. We still have a few hours of sunlight, so let us find some place to settle for now."

With himself in the lead, and Renir and Elia bringing up the rear, the group set out for the path Braen thought—prayed—other travelers would use. He hadn't wanted this. Not the running, not the leading, not any of it. His grandfather had been a natural ruler, but Braen had spent all his own life avoiding attention, partly to watch from the shadows and partly to escape his father's notice. Not that any of it did any good now.

After an hour, the group reached a fork in the path. The western path most likely led toward the coast and the West Aran Sea. The southern path continued to the mountains and, inevitably, Sunderlind. Braen led them another half hour south before finding a good place to set up camp. It wasn't quite large enough for their number, but it would have to do.

"Set up camp," he ordered. "Renir, I need to speak with you."

While everyone got to work, Renir joined Braen off to the side.

"We will need more food than what people brought with them. Take two hunters and see what you can find."

"Understood."

Braen waited until Renir and two men left before jumping in to help with the camp preparations. At least with more food, maybe the people wouldn't revolt. He hoped so, anyway. He had no idea how to be a leader, but he figured he had no choice now. His people needed him.

Chapter Eleven

"Where is my sister?"

Servants exchanged glances before one spoke up. "Queen Furia is in her chambers, Lady Lerian. May I—"

"No. I will speak with her. You are dismissed."

"Remind me to never turn my back on her."

Micheil nodded. "A lot has changed since you were here last."

Soren Krelius had arrived not long after the midday meal. Micheil instantly remembered him, though. The mage stood just a few inches shorter than Micheil, with a head full of long, dark chestnut hair and pale green eyes that seemed to watch everything all at once. Soren, in his youth, had been a bit of an imp, always finding ways to get into trouble. Micheil just hadn't been able to put the name to the face until now.

Soren turned to him. "Whispers run as rampant here as they always have. How is she?"

Micheil gestured toward the hallway that led to his own chambers. "Her mind has been preoccupied lately, understandably so. Breasal used magic in the conception, so she is progressing faster than normal."

"What is her plan for the child?"

"I don't know yet." Micheil stopped outside his door. "Soren, I know Vala told you to apply to the guild, but I need you here."

Soren chuckled. "Vala was a good teacher, but I make my own path. I don't think she cared for my lack of obedience. My duty is to the throne. What do you require of me?"

Micheil opened the door and gestured for Soren to enter. Once they were alone, he continued. "I don't trust Lerian. I don't think many people do. She knows Furia is pregnant, but not by whom. Lerian will no doubt find a way to take over the throne, and that can't happen."

"What are our options?"

"Our only other choice is Vanya."

"Vanya?" Soren wandered over to the window that looked down onto the courtyard. "The only Vanya I recall is a soldier, an archer more likely to put an arrow between an enemy's eyes than play diplomat." He turned to Micheil. "Are we talking about the same woman?"

"Indeed."

Soren joined Micheil at the table and nodded in thanks when Micheil handed him a cup of wine. "What can I do?"

"Help me keep an eye on Lerian, for Furia's sake. I don't know what Breasal did to speed up the pregnancy, but the moment the child arrives, I must get him out of Cypravion."

"Where will you go?"

"Akuron," Micheil said. "There is a couple I know very well, have known for quite some time. They have no children of their own but long for one. I'll take the baby to them."

"And the queen is okay with this?"

"It was her idea to get him away from here. She fears for his safety. The spell to conceal his parentage is permanent, but Furia feels it's necessary to take him elsewhere regardless. I can't say I disagree."

Soren finished his wine and stood. "I assume you wish me to remain in the palace?"

"I would appreciate it," Micheil said. "Mari had servants prepare your room. As I said: keep an eye on Lerian. I trust her as much as I trust Vala."

Soren chuckled. "Noted. I will do so."

Micheil got up to see Soren out, but the moment he opened the door, a whirlwind of fury and long red hair burst into his room. He and Soren barely had time to move, lest Vanya skewer them both. She spun around, green eyes smoldering with anger.

"I'm going to—"

Micheil gestured to Soren. "Vanya, may I introduce Soren Krelius? Soren, this well-armed tempest is Vanya, heir to the throne whether she likes it or not."

Vanya blinked and, for the first time in Micheil's recollection, seemed at a loss for words.

Soren lifted her hand and kissed the top of it. "It's a pleasure, my lady."

"I was just going to show Soren to his room," Micheil said. "Did you need me?"

Vanya shook her head. "I just needed to vent before I kill my mother's sister."

Soren snorted. "You and many others, I imagine. I caught a glimpse in the throne room, and I was not impressed."

"So you see why I despise her," Vanya said.

"I do." Soren offered his arm.

Vanya, much to Micheil's surprise, accepted. Micheil led them down the hall to Soren's room. When he turned, he managed to keep a neutral expression at the sight of Vanya actually smiling. He couldn't recall the last time he'd seen her do so.

Perhaps Soren's presence would be more beneficial than Micheil had originally thought.

* * *

"You looked puzzled."

"That's putting it mildly." Micheil looked up from the book he'd been reading. Nothing he'd found could explain the connection he now had with Furia's unborn child. The idea unnerved him more than he cared to admit—even to himself. "I didn't expect to see you so soon."

Taeral glanced down the hall from where he stood in the doorway, then back to Micheil. "We are leaving. Word from Midland has reached us. Something is going on in Ronu Wood."

"Breasal?"

"That would be my guess."

Micheil sighed. "I fear this is only the beginning."

Taeral toyed with the helmet in his hand for a moment before speaking. "Micheil..."

"I know." Micheil walked over and gave the man, who'd been his lover for the past several months, a tremulous smile. "You sense it, too."

"What is it?" Taeral asked him. "What happened?"

Micheil wasn't sure how to explain any of it. "In all honesty, I have no idea. All I can tell you is that, when I did the ritual for Furia, something... connected me to the child. I can't stay here, and neither can he."

Taeral nodded. "I'd say I understand, but I don't. Magic has never made much sense to me. But I know you well, and I know you're a man of your word. If your duty now lies with protecting this child, then I have no doubt you will do everything in your power to keep him safe."

Micheil took a final kiss, knowing he'd most likely not see Taeral again. A soldier's life was never one of certainty, and

Micheil had no choice but to leave for Akuron. "Rest assured, I have enjoyed every moment we have had."

"As have I," Taeral said with a smile. "Stay safe."

Micheil would've said the same, but with war looming, it held little weight. "Thank you. For everything."

He watched Taeral walk away, a small, dull ache following. It hadn't been love, but there was affection. Taeral disappeared around a corner, and Micheil returned to perusing the pile of books he'd dug out of the bowels of the guild library.

Nothing. He'd found absolutely nothing on such erratic connections after spells. It should've been a simple but permanent glamour. He had the distinct feeling it went far deeper, though. Certainly more than he ever intended.

He closed the last book and sat back in his chair. The sun had set a few hours ago, and he'd yet to finish his dinner Mari had brought in earlier. As he nibbled on an apple slice, he thought of the coming days.

The Ysindrocs were a middle-aged couple he'd befriended nearly ten years ago. Unlike many other humans, they were humble and didn't care that he was an elf. They'd been trying for years to have children, and not even his own magic had helped. He prayed they wouldn't question him on the baby's heritage—for the babe's sake and theirs.

Epilogue

Five months later...

"I want to see him."

"Your Highness—"

Furia continued on toward the front gate, ignoring every word Micheil said. Were she not his queen, he wouldn't have hesitated to stop her with magic the moment she walked out the palace doors. Whatever hold Breasal had on her was stronger than anything Micheil had ever encountered. He had no choice but to follow her. The pregnancy had progressed at an alarming rate, and she was due to give birth any day now.

"I understand your misgivings, but I am quite capable," she protested as if this were nothing more than a ride through the relatively safe woods of Cypravion. "Send guards, if you feel you must."

He stopped and sighed. He couldn't leave the capital without someone to run it, and he couldn't force her to stay. He hurried back to the stables and shouted for guards before he even dismounted. Several rushed to his side.

"Stay with her, do not let her out of your sight," he ordered. "If that Koleri bastard harms a single hair on her head, kill him."

The guards mounted their own horses and swiftly joined Furia on her ill-advised trek to visit Breasal. Nothing good would come of this.

Micheil returned to the palace. He needed to keep watch on things in Akuron. As much as he disliked the idea, his only choice was to put Vanya back on the throne as regent. He could already hear her vehement protests.

* * *

"Something is very wrong."

Elia and Renir looked at Braen, but he ignored the unspoken questions. He'd felt the change, a shift in the air, the flush that rain through his dragon-tainted blood.

"We need to return."

"But—"

He cut Renir off. "My father has done something terrible. I can feel it like I feel the cold in these damned mountains. Lead the people into Sunderlind. I have to go back."

As Elia, Renir, and several others began breaking down camp, Braen wandered to the cave's entrance. It had been big enough for them all and provided shelter from the cold and rain. Situated high on the mountainside, it afforded a good view of the lands below, including Ronu Wood where his father's palace sat nestled among the trees. Then he spotted it: a plume of smoke beginning to rise from the dense forest. Another sprang up a moment later.

"What is that?" Elia asked when she and Renir joined him.

Murmurs started rippling through their group as others gathered to watch the smoke.

"My father ensuring only those loyal remain with him. I have to get everyone out before he kills them all." Braen turned to Renir and Elia. "Get these people far away from here. Now."

* * *

For several hours after Furia's departure, the throne sat eerily silent. Micheil remained in his own seat, present for anything that needed his attention, but his own chaotic thoughts refused to settle down. Something felt off, but he couldn't pinpoint it. Perhaps he should've used magic to stop her, consequences be damned.

Vanya entered the room but stopped short of actually sitting on the throne that would one day be hers. "Remind me to put an arrow through that bastard's head when I finally meet him."

"I certainly wouldn't stop you."

"Why did she go back to him?"

"He has a spell over her that not even I can counter," Micheil said. He stood and left the dais, wandering over to a window that looked out onto the courtyard.

"Micheil—" Vanya started.

Shouts came from beyond the palace doors. A moment later, a guard burst through them.

"Master Thierauf! There are reports coming in from Akuron. King Breasal is killing all who oppose him."

"Assemble our soldiers. We are officially at war." Micheil turned to Vanya, who glared at him from where she stood in front of the throne.

"I should be out there!"

"I need you here," he said with as much calm as he could muster.

"I'm a soldier!"

"You're also heir to the throne!" he shouted. "I will bring her home, but we can't leave the throne empty. Her sister will gladly take over and destroy everything your mother worked so hard for, Vanya. Please trust me. Soren will remain by your side should you need him, but I have to go."

She scowled but dropped down onto the seat. "Fine. Bring her back."

Micheil left without another word. He met Mari in the stables, and she handed him his chainmail shirt. "I'll return as soon as I can."

"Micheil," she said, hand on his arm, "please be careful."

He wanted to remind her that war was never careful, but he didn't. He just kissed her forehead and tugged on the chain shirt before mounting Aserion. He took his sword from Mari and urged Aserion onward to join the soldiers leaving the city in a steady stream. His only thought was to get Furia back and kill the bastard who now threatened all of Socendor.

* * *

"You have created an abomination!"

"I have created a *god*."

"How dare you toy with fate!"

Furia's cheek stung from the vicious strike. Tears filled her eyes, but she refused to give the devil the satisfaction of seeing them. She flinched when he reached out once more, but this time, the touch was deceptively gentle.

"He is my son." Breasal's ebony fingers traced the line of Furia's jaw, down to the pulse point of her throat. His red eyes held her captive.

"Yes, my lord," she whispered.

Breasal smiled.

She had thought the sorcerer beautiful—deadly, but beautiful. But Breasal was a monster. The knowledge that she had given birth to his child broke her heart. He'd sworn his magic only ensured the child would be a boy, to carry on his line. The truth, she'd discovered, was far more insidious: the magic also carried Breasal's terrible power. Should the child survive, he would be hunted all his life.

"You are dismissed," Breasal commanded with a dismissive wave. "I will summon you if I desire your presence."

Furia bowed and backed out of the room. Several paces from the door, she turned and hurried down the dim corridor. She'd welcomed the sorcerer into her bed once. Now she knew never to turn her back to him.

Shouts echoed from the far end of the hall, and several servants rushed toward her. As they neared, she saw horror and fear etched into their expressions.

"My Lady!" One of the servants grabbed Furia's arm and tugged her, giving Furia no choice but to join the steady stream of people rushing toward the front of the castle.

The distinct sounds of fighting kept pace with them. Furia dared a glance backward. Several of Breasal's guards were gaining on Furia and the others. One of the ladies screamed as a soldier caught her. Blood splattered on the stone walls and floor, galvanizing everyone to move faster.

Before they reached the outer hall, the main doors of the keep burst inward. Elven swordsmen and archers spilled into the entryway. Some ushered Furia and the servants out of the keep.

Furia spotted a familiar face. "What is happening?"

Micheil scowled toward the throne room. "Get to safety, Your Highness. Breasal has murdered many Koleri who oppose him. He will answer for his crimes."

Thunder shook the keep, and a roar echoed from inside the throne room a moment before the throne room doors splintered outward, taking several servants' lives. Furia screamed and ducked as a shattered wooden beam narrowly missed her.

"Where is the baby?"

"Hidden. He used magic to... make him come now. I don't know how, Micheil."

Anther scream pierced through the din of battle. Micheil grabbed her arm. "Get out! Get him and leave this place!"

Furia rushed through the crowd, praying her child still remained unseen in the old oak's hollow trunk. She spotted it in the distance, relieved Micheil's magic shielded the baby's true identity. He had been born as dark as his father, but Micheil's glamour masked it moments after birth. If anyone knew...

Pain lanced through her body, and she stumbled to a halt. A blade protruded from her breast.

"Did you think I would let you go?" Breasal withdrew his sword and circled her. "Where are you going, my dear? Where is my son?"

Blood spilled down her dress, and she dropped to her knees. She stared up at him. "Safe from you."

"No matter." Breasal lifted the sword once more. "I *will* find him."

* * *

"Where is the queen?"

A servant pointed toward the enclosed courtyard of Breasal's palace. Micheil pushed his way through the confused mass of soldiers and commonfolk. Breasal had not been in the throne room when Micheil and the others finally made it into the vast hall. Micheil left the soldiers to hunt down the bastard and set his own sights on getting Furia and the baby out before Breasal could find them.

He heard shouting and hurried down the corridor. The moment he stepped into the courtyard, Furia's head tumbled to the ground. Micheil gave Breasal no time to react. He swung his own sword, giving the bastard the same death. Breasal's headless body dropped to the ground in a puddle of sizzling blood. Micheil kicked the severed head across the courtyard where it landed at the feet of the tyrant's bastard son.

"I have no qualms with you," Micheil said.

"You did me—and Socendor—an enormous service. Take the child and go. I have to get everyone I can out of this place," Braen said.

Micheil nodded and, from deep within a hollowed oak, withdrew an infant. The baby, whose father had been a Koleri, now looked like a mortal child. Micheil cradled him close. The others were dealing with the last of Breasal's men, which gave Micheil time to get the infant away. Micheil prayed the boy would never find out his true heritage.

When the shouting began to fade, Micheil peered around the corner of the building he stood against. Soldiers and people with carts carried the dead away, and many others set about clearing the palace. If this child was to survive, it wouldn't be here. Micheil slipped around the building. He let out a low whistle, and Aserion whinnied in reply. A moment later, the stallion joined Micheil. Aserion stood patiently while Micheil got settled with the baby cradled in one arm.

"Quietly now, we are going to Akuron."

Aserion snorted softly and picked his way along the backs of the buildings, keeping well out of sight. Micheil let the stallion guide them to safety from this place. Once they left the area,

Micheil cast a glamour on himself. To anyone human, he appeared as one of them now.

He lost track of time, his mind whirling. He couldn't return to Seriete. His duty now lay in the crook of his left arm, bundled and shielded from the outside world.

By the time they reached the city of Akuron Heights, the sun had completely set. The streets were empty, and a somber mood lay over the place. Akuron Heights had been under human-only rule for ages, and they'd managed to avoid Breasal's direct wrath. With the Koleri king dead, it left King Andrion to expand his own control all the way to the mountains, including Ronu Wood.

Micheil halted Aserion outside the town smithy and dismounted with the baby in his arms. He stepped through the open door and met the welcoming smiles of the only humans he ever really cared for: Emil and Myra Ysindroc.

"Micheil!" Myra jumped up to embrace him, but she froze when she saw the baby. "Oh, my..."

Micheil handed the child to her. "An orphan. I trust no one else to care for him."

Myra took the infant and held him. "He's perfect," she whispered. Tears wet the child's dark hair.

Emil stood and smiled down at their new baby. He looked up at Micheil. "Thank you. I didn't think our prayers for children would ever be answered."

"You are both quite welcome. His heritage is unknown," Micheil lied. "But it is of no matter now. He is your son. I am going to offer my services to the king. Should you need me, you know I will always be here."

The Ysindrocs hugged him, and Myra kissed his cheek. Goodbyes said, Micheil glanced once last time at the child. Mesmerizing green eyes met his own, and a shiver raced along Micheil's spine. This child's story was not over.

About the Author

Katherine Cook has been an avid fantasy nut all her life, and she places the "blame" squarely on J.R.R. Tolkien. At the age of nine, she devoured The Hobbit and the entire Lord of the Rings trilogy. She never looked back.

Katherine Cook is the alter ego of gay romance author Mychael Black and het romance author Carys Seraphine.

Read more at https://katherinecookauthor.com/.